The Adventures of Lucky Duck

ISBN 979-8-89112-348-9 (Hardcover)
ISBN 979-8-89112-347-2 (Digital)

Covenant Books
11661 Hwy 707
Murrells Inlet, SC 29576
www.covenantbooks.com

The Adventures of Lucky Duck

Lucky Duck and Friends' Jeep Adventures

DeDe Gale

1

Hi! My name is Lucky…Lucky Duck. Boy, do I have a story to share with you! I currently live in the Texas Hill Country, where some people believe it's the greatest place on earth. When the wildflowers are in bloom in spring, all you can see is a sea of bluebonnets, Indian paintbrushes, and black-eyed Susans. It is a beautiful sight!

I am a relatively good-looking dude, at least that is what my mama tells me. I am your basic yellow ducky, but the rest of my *getup* is what makes me who I am! I wear a ten-gallon Stetson cowboy hat and a red bandana around my neck. I have some leather cowboy boots that I had specially made to fit my flippers, and I top the whole look off with a leather vest with conchos and fringe. The chicks sure do dig it!

My adventures started about three years ago when my mom had a really bad day. She had a very unpleasant encounter with someone that was not very nice to her. We were all shocked! Mama had always taught me and my brothers and sisters that we should treat others as we would want to be treated. She called it the golden rule! So, to see her sad because someone else didn't have the same teaching was very disappointing to us all.

After the disagreement was all said and done, we really didn't know what was going to happen next. Mama thought long and hard about how she felt and what she was going to do about it. All of a sudden, it was like a light bulb came on! She looked at me and said, "Lucky, I think that right now is a perfect time for me to turn this into a teaching moment for you. I want to show you what it truly means to live by the golden rule!"

I guess now is as good a time as any to tell you that my mom is the coolest duck of them all! She is a card-carrying member of the Jeep tribe! She drives a silver Jeep Wrangler with blue accents, soft-top of course, to make it easy to go topless on those beautiful spring and fall days. Its cute little round lights and slick grill make it turn heads everywhere we go!

As we cruised around that day, it wasn't long before she found a parking lot with another *sweet* Jeep just sitting there minding its own business. It was a ruby-red Rubicon with shiny rims and tread that looked like it could climb to the top of Mt. Everest! Mom pulled up and parked right beside it because that is what you do when you are part of the tribe! Whenever you find a Jeep, there is usually another one not too far away!

We were both just enjoying the moment when Mama looked at me and said, "Okay, Lucky, it's time to do your thing! Let's show the world what it means to do unto others as you would have them do unto you!" Mama picked me up and sat me right on the door handle of that Jeep Wrangler!

I was kind of thinking, *What do I do now?* I didn't have to wait long before the owner came out of the store and walked toward her Jeep. As she approached us and saw me sitting there on her door handle, she broke out into the prettiest smile you ever saw, and all because of me?

It made me feel so good on the inside that I broke out into a big 'ol goofy smile as well. She whipped out her phone and took a picture of me sitting there...grinning like a fool!

As we drove away that day, I will always remember the beautiful smile on my mama's face as she waved goodbye to me. I soon learned that the owner of that ruby-red Rubicon was Rebecca. We became the best of buds from that day on. She took me and put me in my new place of honor...right up there on the dash! What a view! I could see everywhere and everything, including all the other Jeeps that we passed. And you know what else? Just about everyone that passed us waved at me! It's like they know me!

Rebecca was so happy to have received me that she now shares joy and happiness by giving other Jeep owners some of my friends and family as well. In fact, it's like the whole world is duck, duck, jeeping! No matter what state or country you are in anymore, just look around. There are Jeeps and ducks *everywhere*! And when you ask about it, you usually hear, "It's just a Jeep thing!"

Mama shared a wonderful gift with me that day. She taught me that people (and ducks too) can fulfill their destiny of making those around them happy by giving of themselves. You see, you never know what someone else is going through in their life, and a simple act of kindness can make all the difference in the world. Sharing smiles was my destiny, and I am living a truly blessed life, just like the luckiest duck in the world!

(Stay tuned for more Lucky Duck and friends' Jeep adventures!)

About the Author

DeDe Gale was born and bred in the great state of Texas. She lives in the Hill Country with her wonderful husband of thirty years and their pack of canine companions! She received her master's degree in public administration and bachelor of science degree in justice administration from Wayland Baptist University.

After a rewarding career in the criminal justice field, it was time to let her inner child out to play. She was inspired to write her first children's book from the colorful display of rubber ducks that live on the dash of her Jeep Wrangler. Their adorable personalities come to life in her series of books centered around the popular jeep ducking craze, spreading like wildfire across the country.

DeDe enjoys a multitude of hobbies, including fishing, reading, and swimming, or just about any adventure that leads to fun! Seeing the world from the front seat of her Wrangler is what it is all about. Life is best shared with family and friends, which she is gratefully blessed with an abundance of.

Printed in the USA
CPSIA information can be obtained
at www.ICGtesting.com
LVHW051946130824
788121LV00003B/31